1914
Rebecca
AND THE MOVIES

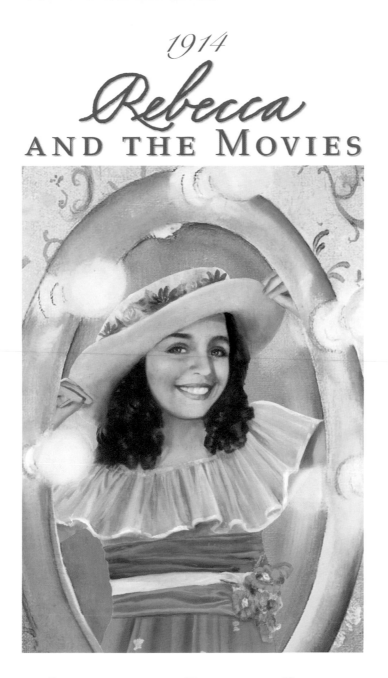

BY JACQUELINE DEMBAR GREENE

ILLUSTRATIONS ROBERT HUNT

VIGNETTES SUSAN MCALILEY

★ American Girl®

THE AMERICAN GIRLS

 1764   KAYA, an adventurous Nez Perce girl whose deep love for horses and respect for nature nourish her spirit

1774   FELICITY, a spunky, spritely colonial girl, full of energy and independence

 1824   JOSEFINA, a Hispanic girl whose heart and hopes are as big as the New Mexico sky

1854   KIRSTEN, a pioneer girl of strength and spirit who settles on the frontier

 1864   ADDY, a courageous girl determined to be free in the midst of the Civil War

1904  SAMANTHA, a bright Victorian beauty, an orphan raised by her wealthy grandmother

1914  REBECCA, a lively girl with dramatic flair growing up in New York City

1934  KIT, a clever, resourceful girl facing the Great Depression with spirit and determination

1944  MOLLY, who schemes and dreams on the home front during World War Two

  JULIE, a fun-loving girl from San Francisco who faces big changes—and creates a few of her own

Published by American Girl Publishing, Inc.
Copyright © 2009 by American Girl, LLC

Questions or comments? Call 1-800-845-0005, visit **americangirl.com**,
or write to Customer Service, American Girl, 8400 Fairway Place,
Middleton, WI 53562-0497.

Printed in China
09 10 11 12 13 14 LEO 10 9 8 7 6 5 4 3 2 1

PICTURE CREDITS
The following individuals and organizations have generously given permission
to reprint images contained in "Looking Back": pp. 72–73—Karnofsky family, Drexler family,
courtesy of Miriam D. Frankel; Library of Congress (leapfrog); The Granger Collection (stickball);
© Bettmann/Corbis (ice wagon); pp. 74–75—Brown Brothers (theater entryway); © Corbis
(title card); © Bettmann/Corbis (John Barrymore); Culver Pictures (Theda Bara); pp. 76–77—
Thanhouser Company Film Preservation, Inc. (Helen Badgely); Los Angeles Public Library
(Mary Pickford movie set); © Richard T. Nowitz/Corbis (girls in theater).

Cataloging-in-Publication Data available from Library of Congress

TO MY FATHER, GEORGE DEMBAR,
AND TO JULIE, GLORIA, SHIRLEE, AND JACK
FOR SHARING THEIR MEMORIES

Rebecca's parents and grand-parents came to America before Rebecca was born, along with millions of other Jewish immigrants from different parts of the world. These immigrants brought with them many different traditions and ways of being Jewish. Practices varied widely between families, and differences among Jewish families were just as common in Rebecca's time as they are today. Rebecca's stories show the way one Jewish family could have lived in 1914 and 1915.

Rebecca's grandparents spoke mostly *Yiddish*, a language that was common among Jews from Eastern Europe. For help in pronouncing or understanding the foreign words in this book, look in the glossary on page 78.

TABLE OF CONTENTS

REBECCA'S FAMILY AND FRIENDS

REBECCA'S FAMILY

PAPA
Rebecca's father, an understanding man who owns a small shoe store

MAMA
Rebecca's mother, who keeps a good Jewish home—and a good sense of humor

REBECCA
A lively girl with dramatic flair, growing up in New York City

SADIE AND SOPHIE
Rebecca's twin sisters, who like to remind Rebecca that they are fourteen

BENNY AND VICTOR
Rebecca's brothers, who are five and twelve

GRANDPA
*Rebecca's grandfather,
an immigrant from
Russia who carries on
the Jewish traditions*

BUBBIE
*Rebecca's grandmother,
an immigrant from
Russia who is feisty
and outspoken*

ROSE
*A wise girl who is
Rebecca's good friend*

MAX
*Mama's cousin, who
leads the exciting life
of an actor*

LILY
*A movie star who doesn't
shy away from new roles,
onscreen and in life*

MAX'S
MAGIC

Mr. Goldberg cranked the handle on the phonograph in his candy shop, and the bright, tinkly sound of a piano filled the store. A singer's voice crooned,

> *Come on and hear, come on and hear*
> *Alexander's Ragtime Band.*
> *Come on and hear, come on and hear,*
> *It's the best band in the land!*

Rebecca hummed along, and her friend Rose snapped her fingers in time to the lively music.

"Isn't it swell to hear records?" Rebecca asked. "Just think—if we had a phonograph, we could play music whenever we wanted."

The tempo of the song slowed as the machine wound down. Mr. Goldberg put on a new record and cranked the handle.

Rebecca headed toward the door. "We'd better go."

"Oh, not yet!" Rose protested. She clung to Rebecca's arm. "Let's hear the next song."

"I think we've hung around long enough without buying anything," Rebecca whispered. "I don't want to annoy Mr. Goldberg."

"I don't think he minds," Rose said. "It's awfully quiet in here for a Saturday afternoon." Only two customers sat on swiveling stools, sipping frothy egg creams. "Since this week is Passover, I guess hardly anybody is eating out." Rose looked longingly at jars filled with brightly colored jelly beans. "I sure would love a handful of those." She followed reluctantly as Rebecca held the door open.

"So would I," Rebecca said, "but Mama won't even let me order a soda. There are so many foods we can't eat during Passover, she and Bubbie don't trust anything they haven't made in their own kitchens."

The girls strolled up the street, enjoying the sunshine that warmed the spring afternoon. Rose shrugged. "Still, it's fun eating the special Passover foods we have only once a year, like *matzo*. Don't you think so?"

matzo

"Usually I do," Rebecca agreed. "Except for this year." She hesitated a moment. "Tomorrow's my birthday."

"Oooh—your birthday!" Rose exclaimed. "That is one of the best things in America. Back in Russia, my family never celebrated birthdays—not like here. Are you going to have a party?"

Rebecca scuffed her shoes along the sidewalk. "That's the problem—we've been so busy cleaning and cooking for Passover, I think everyone has forgotten." She kicked at a pebble and added glumly, "Anyway, I couldn't have a birthday cake unless it was as flat as matzo! What fun is a birthday without a big, fluffy cake?"

"Oh, Rebecca," Rose said, putting her arm around her friend, "how awful. No party, and no cake either. Well, if you're not having a party this year, then next year I think you should have two!"

Rebecca knew that her friend was trying to

3

cheer her up. She forced a small smile.

"Let's walk the long way to your house and see what's playing at the movie theater," Rose said. She steered Rebecca down a side street, whistling "Alexander's Ragtime Band" as she walked.

"What a boring day," Rebecca grumbled. "First we go to the candy store, where I can't even order a soda, and now to the movies, which my parents say I'm too young to see."

"It's fun looking at the posters, though," Rose said. "Don't you love seeing the beautiful actresses?"

The girls ducked around a gang of boys playing stickball and passed some girls playing jacks on the sidewalk. In a few more blocks, they came to the marble columns of the Orpheum Photo Play Theater. Giant letters blazed across the golden marquee: "Lillian Armstrong in *Cleopatra*."

Rebecca felt a cool rush of air as she and Rose stepped into the shade under the marquee. It gave Rebecca shivers to be so close to the theater. She still remembered the afternoon last fall when Max had brought the entire family to see a Charlie Chaplin movie. It was the first and only time her parents had let her attend. When the theater lights dimmed and the show began, Rebecca had felt an excitement like nothing before. It was astonishing to see pictures moving on a screen.

"Look at this!" Rose exclaimed. Rebecca gazed at the posters in gilded frames on either side of the entrance. A sultry actress with shadowed eyes outlined in black stared boldly out at them. Her straight hair was adorned with a golden headdress. She wore a low-cut dress and held an open-mouthed snake close to her chest.

"My family would especially never let me see this one!" Rebecca croaked. "It looks scary!"

"But it's about a real person," Rose said. "It's the story of Cleopatra, who was queen of Egypt. It's about history!"

"Try telling that to Bubbie," Rebecca muttered. "Maybe she'd let me go to the movies if they made one about the history of Passover, when the Jews escaped from slavery in Egypt." She pretended to be a barker calling people to the theater. She cupped her hands around her mouth and called in a husky voice, "See Moses lead his people to freedom! Watch as the Jews flee across the desert with nothing to eat but unleavened bread!"

*"My family would especially never let
me see this one!" Rebecca croaked. "It looks scary!"*

"You know, that's not a bad idea," Rose remarked. "You should tell your cousin Max. Isn't he a movie actor?"

Rebecca nodded. "The best part would show how the Jews couldn't get across the Red Sea. The Pharaoh's soldiers would be right behind them, and the Jews would be sure they're going to be captured. But Moses raises his staff, and the sea parts as the Jews rush across safely." She raised her arms in a sweeping gesture. "Let my people go!" she recited in a deep voice, as if she were playing the role of Moses.

"That would make a thrilling moving picture," Rose agreed, "as long as God parted the sea again for the filming."

"Come on," Rebecca said. "It's getting late."

But Rose lingered under the marquee, reading all the posters out loud. She pointed to the glamorous poster of Lillian Armstrong. "I don't think I've heard of this Cleopatra actress before."

"She must be new," said Rebecca. "I haven't seen her in a motion picture magazine. Of course, I only get to see the ones I can sneak away from my sisters."

The air was turning cooler. "We really should go," Rebecca insisted. At last, Rose headed back to the sidewalk and ambled along toward Rebecca's row house, stopping to admire the window displays in the stores along the route. The girls paused at a tempting array of pastries and cakes in the window of an Italian bakery.

"You'd think that even at Passover, it would be okay to have a birthday cake," Rebecca blurted out. "I mean, Moses led the Jews out of Egypt thousands of years ago. We know they escaped without enough time to let their bread rise, and the unleavened bread was baked into flat matzos—but why do we have to worry about it today?"

"To remember how hard life was when the Jews were slaves," Rose said. "Eating matzos instead of bread and cake helps us remember our ancestors."

Rebecca felt a twinge of guilt. Mama and Bubbie had cooked for days to prepare the *seders,* the festive Passover meals they shared on the first two nights. The seders were feasts of delicious foods that followed a retelling of the Jews' journey out of Egypt to freedom. Passover was one of the most important Jewish holidays.

"It's probably wrong to even wish for a cake," Rebecca confessed. "I guess I just have to skip my birthday this year."

"Think about something fun," Rose suggested as they approached Rebecca's building. "I know— let's play hopscotch. Do you have any chalk?"

"I don't really feel like it," Rebecca said, heading up the front stoop.

"Well, let's just sit outside for a while, then," Rose said, plopping herself down on the top step.

"It's too chilly," Rebecca said, pulling Rose up.

Rose followed Rebecca into the kitchen, but the apartment was strangely quiet. "Oh, it's you, Rebecca! You're home already?" Mama asked, hastily throwing a napkin over a plate. "Everyone's out playing," Mama added before Rebecca had even asked. "I've got to take this upstairs to Bubbie." She picked up the covered dish and headed out the door.

"I'm hungry," Rebecca said when Mama had left. She looked in the icebox, but there was nothing except a jar of cold leftover soup. Rebecca sighed. She took a piece of matzo from a basket on the table and offered one to Rose. "Do you want jam on it?" she asked.

icebox

9

Rose shook her head. "I've got an idea—let's go up and give the pigeons a taste. I wonder if they like matzo."

Rebecca smiled at the thought. "Good idea!" She  loved feeding the pigeons that the janitor kept in cages on the rooftop.

As the girls stepped into the hallway, Rebecca heard Bubbie calling from the top landing. "Rebecca! Come by me for a minute." Rebecca sighed. She couldn't think of any chores she might have forgotten. She peered up the stairwell.

"Come, *bubeleh*," her grandmother said, using her favorite Yiddish word for "sweetie." "I need some help."

Rebecca took a few steps up. "Can I come up later?" she called. "My friend Rose is here."

"So, you'll both come," Bubbie said. "Hurry, now." Rebecca climbed the stairs, her feet dragging. Rose followed a few steps behind her.

Bubbie smiled, her eyes crinkling at the corners as she nudged Rebecca inside. What was Bubbie so pleased about?

"Rose and I were—" Rebecca started to explain,

but before she could finish, a chorus of voices shouted, "Surprise!"

From behind the furniture, Rebecca's friends Lucy, Gertie, and Sarah all jumped out, along with cousin Ana. Aunt Fannie and Uncle Jacob stepped from behind the bedroom door, laughing. Her cousins Josef and Michael called *"Mazel tov—* congratulations!" Mama and Papa and Rebecca's brothers and sisters were all crowded into the tiny apartment. Rebecca was speechless.

Mama gave her a hug. "Did you really think we'd forget your birthday?" she asked.

Rebecca felt giddy with pleasure. They hadn't forgotten after all. She grinned at Rose. "You knew about the party all along! That's why you kept thinking of excuses not to come back here."

"I could barely keep it secret!" Rose giggled. "You were so glum thinking you couldn't have a party because of Passover."

"What, you think we can't eat because of this holiday?" Bubbie said, passing around a plate of sweets. "Holidays are for eating—and so are birthdays!"

"And we're going to make egg creams for

everyone," Papa announced. He held a blue glass bottle of seltzer, while Grandpa brought out a jar of homemade chocolate syrup.

There was a sharp knock on the door. *Rap-rap-a-tap-tap!* Rebecca knew the code. She ran to the door and gave two taps to complete the rhythm. *Rap-rap!* She pulled open the door, and sure enough, there was cousin Max.

"I hear there's a party with lots of food!" Max stepped into the crowded room. "Come with me, birthday girl," he said, leading Rebecca to a chair. He pulled a flowery scarf from his pocket and draped it around Rebecca's neck. Then he cocked his head to one side. "Hmmm . . . I don't think this is quite right for you," he decided. Making a fist with one hand, he pushed the scarf into it with the other. Everyone watched, mesmerized, as the scarf disappeared.

"It's magic!" Benny exclaimed, clapping his hands.

Max tapped his fist with one finger and slowly said, "Abracadabra!" With a dramatic flick, he opened his hand. The scarf was gone, and in its place there was a pink paper rose.

"Oooh!" cried the group. They gave Max

a round of applause. He bowed, handing Rebecca the flower. She beamed at Max.

Max scratched his head. "I don't know. What good is a rose without anyplace to put it? Hold on . . ."

He retrieved a large round box from the hallway, which he placed in Rebecca's lap. She pulled the lid off and lifted out a cream-colored hat with a huge brim decorated with flowers.

"Goodness gracious!" gasped Mama. She frowned at Max. "I think you've been around theater people too long. Rebecca's only turning ten, you know!"

Max ignored Mama's protest. He tucked the rose in with the other flowers and set the hat on Rebecca's head.

"Oh, Max," Rebecca sighed, "I feel just like a movie star!"

"We have a present for you, too," Sadie said, "although it's not nearly as dramatic as that hat." She handed Rebecca a small envelope. Inside was a colored postcard with a picture of Charlie Chaplin on it. On the back, her sisters had written, "This entitles Rebecca Rubin to one

Charlie Chaplin

13

motion picture show, with an ice cream soda to follow."

Rebecca enfolded her sisters in one big hug. "Do you really mean it?"

"Now that you're ten," Sophie smiled, "we think you're old enough to go to the pictures with us."

Rebecca opened the rest of her presents and thanked everyone. Then Max stood in front of her and arranged the hat brim at a stylish tilt. When he stepped aside, Rebecca peered from under the brim to see Mama holding a big birthday cake, covered in swirly white frosting. Ten candles glowed on top.

"Happy birthday to you," Max began singing, and everyone joined in.

"A cake!" Rebecca cried. She ought to make a wish, but what more could she wish for? She blew the candles out in one breath. "I didn't think there could be a birthday cake on Passover!"

"It's a sponge cake," Mama explained, "made with special matzo flour."

"But how did you get it to rise up so high and fluffy?" Rebecca asked.

"It's easy when you use twelve eggs!" Mama declared.

"Twelve eggs?" Rebecca repeated in disbelief.

"It's extravagant, I know," said Mama, "but it's not every day that your daughter turns ten."

 Grandpa and Papa made fizzy egg creams in tall glasses while Mama served the cake. Everyone ate and laughed. Too soon, the party was over, and people began to leave.

Gertie turned to Rebecca. "Wherever are you going to wear that hat? I don't think Miss Maloney will allow it at school."

"Since it's school vacation this week," Lucy pointed out, "she can wear it at home."

Max frowned. "You can't have a hat like this one and only wear it at home. This hat is meant to be seen." His face lit up. "I've got it! Wear it Monday when I go to work at the motion picture studio."

Rebecca was puzzled. "Why should I wear it when you're at work?" she asked.

"Because you'll be coming with me," Max said. "Movie people can truly appreciate a hat like this!"

Rebecca caught her breath. "Come with you to the picture studio? Will I get to see a movie being made?" She glanced at her sisters. Sadie and Sophie looked positively green with jealousy.

Bubbie cleared her throat. "Just because there is no school doesn't mean pitcher-making place is for a respectable young lady to go. And in such a hat!"

All eyes turned to Max. "I beg to differ, my dear woman," he said with dignity. "All the actresses at the studio are respectable ladies."

"I don't think we should encourage this moving picture nonsense," Papa said.

Bubbie put her hands on her hips. "And *what* she will eat for lunch?"

Grandpa chimed in. "Monday is school vacation, maybe, but is still Passover. Moving-pitcher place doesn't have Passover food."

Rebecca didn't dare argue with Bubbie and Grandpa and Papa, especially in front of everyone. She looked at Mama and pleaded with her eyes.

Mama hesitated a moment and then put her hand on Papa's shoulder. Rebecca held her breath. "I could boil a couple of eggs and give her a banana and some leftover party cookies. And of course"— Rebecca joined in for the last item—"matzo!" she and Mama said in unison.

Mama smiled. "I think it will be all right for her to go with Max just this once. After all, she's not going to turn into an actress just because she visits a movie studio."

17

CHAPTER
TWO
—
A NEW
WORLD

On Monday morning, before anyone else in the household was awake, Rebecca was washed and dressed. She gave her hair one hundred brushstrokes and put on Max's birthday hat, admiring the way the brim framed her face with graceful curves. She quickly ate breakfast and then brushed her teeth until they glistened. After all, today she was going to meet movie actresses, so she wanted to look her very best.

Mama came into the kitchen and set about making lunches for Rebecca and for Papa to take with him to work. When Max bounded up the stairs, Rebecca was ready and waiting, her lunch box in her hand.

Max chattered on about the studio as they hopped onto the speedy subway. Rebecca had heard about the underground trains but never thought she'd be riding in one, zooming under the streets of New York. When it screeched to a stop, she and Max emerged into the sunlight across from the ferry landing.

"Here's our merry band!" Max exclaimed, joining a boisterous group already seated on the boat. Max introduced Rebecca to some of the actors and crew. The actresses wore stylish dresses and hats and had applied lip color and rouge. The actors wore smart suits and jaunty straw hats with colorful hatbands. They all talked about the scenes to be filmed that day, using language Rebecca had never heard before. Her ears perked up as she tried to guess the meaning of "fades," "takes," and "glass plates." She was pretty sure that a glass plate wasn't something to eat from.

As the ferry glided out into the harbor, Rebecca looked back at the skyline. This was the first time she had ever left the city.

The tall buildings that people called skyscrapers loomed above Manhattan. Rebecca had to agree that they truly seemed to scrape the sky. When the boat sailed past the Statue of Liberty, she raced to the railing to gaze at it. The statue's torch glinted against the blue sky.

Rebecca knew that a young Jewish woman had written the poem inscribed on the statue's base. Rebecca had learned the poem in school, and she especially loved the lines that welcomed immigrants like her parents and grandparents to America. "'Give me your tired, your poor, your huddled masses yearning to breathe free,'" she murmured, quoting the poem.

As Rebecca went back to her seat, she noticed a young couple sitting together near the back of the boat. The woman's hat sprouted a single white feather that arched over her head and nestled next to her cheek. She was quite dainty, with a delicate build and the slimmest waist Rebecca had ever seen. But her hair was the most startling thing about her. It wasn't the color, which was a modest brown—it was the length. Under her fitted hat, the woman's hair was cropped short. Bubbie had been worried about the actresses not being "ladies." She would think it perfectly scandalous to see a young woman with her hair bobbed!

Rebecca couldn't stop staring, but the woman was too absorbed in conversation to notice. "See that lady with her hair cut short?" Rebecca whispered to Max. "She looks familiar somehow, but I don't know why."

Max fidgeted with his bow tie. "Ah, yes," he said, "that's our leading lady, the studio's newest shining star, Miss Lillian Armstrong."

"She's Cleopatra!" Rebecca exclaimed. "I saw her on a movie poster at the Orpheum! Her name is on the marquee."

"I'm lucky just to have my name listed in the film credits," Max muttered. "But definitely below hers. I'm not in the same heavenly constellation as Lillian Armstrong. At least, not yet." He looked at the chatting couple. "That swell beside her is none other than Don Herringbone, veteran of stage and screen." The man was short, but he had a lofty manner about him.

Rebecca giggled. "What a funny name—herring bone. I've never seen one in a moving picture, but I see them all the time in jars of pickled fish!"

"'Don Juan' is what I call him," Max said in a low voice. "That's the name of a famous character in a book who always has a different sweetheart. Too bad Lillian doesn't realize she's just part of the adoring crowd to Don Juan."

The ferry horn blew two loud blasts and chugged toward the landing in New Jersey. A deckhand secured the boat and lowered a gangplank to the wooden dock.

"There's our ride," Max said, pointing to a

motor bus idling on the road.

"A subway ride, then the ferry, and now a motor bus," Rebecca said with delight. "And all on my very first trip away from home." It was going to be a day filled with firsts. "I'm going to remember this forever."

"I still remember my journey from Russia to America as if it were yesterday," Max said. "But for me, it was an oxcart from town, then steerage on a ship, and finally the ferry to Manhattan. I thought I had landed in another world."

Rebecca and Max settled onto a stiff bench seat, while the idling motor bus rattled and sputtered. Don Herringbone guided Lillian Armstrong to the back, his hand under her elbow.

"Good morning, ladies and gentlemen," called the bus driver. "Hold on to your hats, and we're off!"

Rebecca reached up and held fast to her new hat, causing chuckles around her. She laughed at her mistake, realizing the bus driver's comment had just been a joke. As the bus bounced along, Rebecca's hat stayed firmly on her head.

"Oooh!" she squealed, as the bus picked up speed.

"Take this little lady to Coney Island," a square-jawed actor advised Max. "She's a natural for the roller coaster!"

Rebecca watched the sunlit roadside speeding by outside the window. They passed a few horse-drawn wagons, but there were no pushcarts, or crowds of shoppers, or kids playing stickball. Instead, Rebecca saw thick stands of trees, and small towns and farm fields appeared and quickly disappeared behind the rumbling bus. There was not a single apartment building nor more than a few stores scattered along the way. Where would you buy pickles and herring? Where was the candy store? It seemed to Rebecca that she was rushing away from everything she knew—almost as if she herself were an immigrant, leaving her old country behind and looking for opportunity in a new and unfamiliar world.

The bus rounded a curve, bumped along a rutted dirt road, and came to a stop in front of a tall iron fence. Molded into the iron gate were the words "Banbury Cross Studios."

"Why, the studio's name is like the Mother Goose rhyme," said Rebecca. "'Ride a cockhorse to Banbury Cross, to see a fine lady upon a white horse.'"

"You never know what you'll see roaming across the studio lot," Max told her, "and a white horse isn't out of the question."

A security guard swung the wide gates open. The bus lumbered along past a series of warehouses and parked in front of a long, wood-shingled building.

"Whoopee!" exclaimed one of the actresses as she stepped off the bus. "Today the director is going to notice me. I feel it in my bones." She waved her ostrich-plumed hat in the air. "L.B., here I come!"

Rebecca tugged at Max's sleeve. "Who's L.B.?"

"None other than the Grand Pooh-Bah himself, Lawrence B. Diamond, director extraordinaire," Max said as he ushered Rebecca into the building's expansive entryway. "When you see him in the studio, you will know instantly who he is."

Corridors led off in three directions. "The dressing rooms are down there," Max pointed. He turned. "Film studios are that-a-way."

Rebecca looked toward the third corridor. "What's down there?" she asked.

"No place we're supposed to be," said Max, "unless nobody sees us." He tiptoed to the entrance and peered down the dark hallway. He motioned to Rebecca, and she imitated him, creeping up behind him as if they were sneaking up on a sleeping giant. "Let's investigate," Max intoned, and Rebecca followed him gamely, tiptoeing all the way.

Max looked up and down the empty corridor, then opened a door labeled Property Room. He whisked Rebecca inside. "Sometimes we're outdoors on location, with real trees and roads and gardens, but most of the time we're indoors and need lots of props to shoot the scene."

"Shoot?" Rebecca repeated. "You use guns?"

"Oh, no," Max laughed. "When the cameraman starts rolling the camera, we call it *shooting*."

Rebecca thought it seemed odd to roll a camera, but not nearly as odd as the room she found herself in. Shelves holding lamps, flowerpots, dishes, glasses, and linens lined the walls. Hat racks, chairs, sofas, and iceboxes were jumbled in every available space. A rickety table held three phonographs, their shiny horns facing different directions. Wooden crates held swords and rifles, and a dummy dressed in a three-piece suit slumped in a corner.

"All this flotsam and jetsam are the props we

26

use in stage sets," Max explained. "And that's Harry," he added, pointing to the dummy. "He's fallen off more cliffs than any other actor, and he never complains."

Rebecca smiled. "He does look rather lonely, though." She walked over to where the mannequin sat and shook his limp hand. "How do you do, Harry?" she said politely. "It's so thrilling for me to meet a real picture star!"

Max grinned. "You've definitely made Harry the happiest movie actor around. He gets even less respect for what he does than the rest of us."

"But everyone loves motion pictures," Rebecca said. "Except for my parents and Bubbie and Grandpa, that is." She looked sheepishly at Max.

"People don't understand what we do," Max said. "They think we just clown around and don't lead respectable lives with a settled home and a steady job."

Max's life was certainly different from her family's, but Rebecca thought it was more exciting, too.

Max pointed to a pile of large gray rocks in a corner. "Could you toss me one of those boulders?

That big one there will do nicely for today's shoot."

Rebecca wanted to help in any way she could, but she didn't think she could lift the heavy rock in front of her. "Gosh, Max, I don't know," she said.

"Go on," Max said. "Everyone around here has to do her share."

Taking a deep breath, Rebecca put her arms around the rock. It felt rough and rather scratchy. She began lifting slowly. Why, it didn't weigh more than an ounce! In fact, it felt hollow inside. She stood up, holding it awkwardly.

"Papier-mâché!" Max grinned. "We've got mountains of 'em."

Rebecca threw the rock to Max. "Catch!" she yelled as the boulder whizzed through the air. Max's arms flailed out wildly. He barely caught the rock as it sailed toward his head.

"I guess I deserved that," he laughed, dropping the fake boulder back onto the pile. He led Rebecca out, closing the door behind them.

"Who's the doll-baby in the scrumptious hat?" said a sweet voice. An actress was walking up the hallway, carrying a brown wig with flowing ringlets.

"This is my cousin, Rebecca Rubin," Max said.

"Rebecca, meet Miss Lillian Armstrong."

Rebecca smiled shyly and found she could barely speak. "Glad to meet you," she managed. Wait until she told Rose that she had met Cleopatra herself!

"I saw you on the bus this morning, didn't I?" Miss Armstrong asked. "Say, how would you like to see me turn from a real girl into a movie actress?"

Rebecca nodded, unable to say a word.

"I'll take this doll-baby with me," Miss Armstrong said to Max. "You need to get ready for the shoot. You know how L.B. feels about actors being punctual."

Max bent down a little and whispered loudly in Rebecca's ear, "Don't let her steal that hat of yours!" With a wink and a wave, he strolled off down the corridor, whistling brightly.

Miss Armstrong opened her dressing room door. Painted on the outside was a shiny gold star with her name in black lettering just underneath. Rebecca wondered if Max had a star painted on his door, too. Inside the small room, the wallpaper was printed with white lilies, and a vase

of fresh lilies perched on the corner of the dressing table. A full-length triple mirror stood in one corner of the room, and an oval mirror with round lights sat on the dressing table. Everywhere she looked, Rebecca saw her own reflection. She couldn't help admiring the effect of her new hat.

"First of all, you must call me Lily," said the actress. "We aren't very formal here." She pointed to an upholstered chaise longue. "Make yourself comfortable." Lily placed the wig on top of a coat tree and kicked off her shoes. She stepped behind a Chinese folding screen and tossed her clothes across the top. A moment later, Lily emerged wearing a long, flowered robe and settled gracefully on a stool at her dressing table. She opened a small case and lined up a row of jars and foil-covered sticks. "My precious greasepaint box," Lily explained. "Without it, I wouldn't have a movie face."

Lily smoothed on cold cream, then squeezed a bit of buff-colored cream from a tube and covered her face until it looked ghostly pale. Next she drew thick black lines around her eyes and brushed inky paste onto her eyelashes. With her pinky finger, she rubbed on ruddy brownish lip color. Finally, she

Lily settled gracefully on a stool at her dressing table.

dusted on a coating of powder and patted it down with a soft rabbit's foot.

"Why do you have to wear all that makeup?" Rebecca asked politely.

"Without it, my face would photograph as a dark shadow. And after I make my skin so pale, I've got to darken around my eyes, or they wouldn't show up at all." Lily seemed to know that the makeup made her look rather ghoulish. She made a witchy cackle and clawed at the air with her fingers. "Now I've got you in my clutches!" she teased. Rebecca gave a mock scream and shrank back, giggling.

"I know I look odd," Lily admitted, "but it all comes out bright and natural on film." She turned to the mirror again and wrapped a thin scarf around her head. "And this hair bob is perfect for me—so much easier to tuck under a wig." She waved her arm dramatically. "And, doll-baby, I'm always in a wig!"

So there was a reason for the actress's short hair. How could Bubbie argue with that?

A light knock sounded on the door. "*Entrez!*" Lily called. A plump woman came in with an evening gown draped over her arm.

"My dress!" Lily exclaimed. "Mabel, you're a wonder." To Rebecca she said, "I think Mabel could fit an elephant and then remake the dress for a mouse!"

"And in this case, you're the mouse," the dressmaker said, smiling. "It's all nipped in around the waist now." Lily dropped her dressing robe on the floor and held her arms straight up in the air. Mabel pulled the dress over the actress's head. It swished down around Lily's dainty ankles, and Mabel began looping tiny buttons at the back. She pulled and smoothed at the fabric until it hung perfectly.

"Now for your hair," Mabel said. Lily sat down as Mabel fitted the wig onto Lily's head. In spite of the strange makeup, she looked stunning.

"You look like a painting," Rebecca murmured in admiration.

Lily smiled, her teeth pearly white behind the dark lip paint. "I'm playing the daughter of a wealthy society family," she said. "We are about to host a swell social affair. Of course, we'll start with cocktails on the lawn."

Mabel laughed. "That depends on whether or not the set designers painted you a lawn!"

Lily strapped on a pair of delicate shoes that were more elegant than any in Papa's shoe store. Mabel picked up the clothes Lily had left strewn about. She clucked her disapproval, just as Bubbie would have, but Lily didn't seem to notice.

"Shall we?" Lily asked, offering her arm to Rebecca. Together they walked toward the set.

"What else happens in the scene?" Rebecca asked.

"Well, my parents have chosen a rich man for me to marry, but I don't like him." She stamped her tiny foot and frowned until her dark penciled eyebrows nearly touched. "He's vile! I would rather die than marry such a cad!" She changed her expression to a dreamy look and sighed deeply. "I'm secretly in love with the gardener. Of course, my parents wouldn't ever approve, and there's the plot."

Rebecca thought the story sounded a lot like real life. In fact, it sounded a bit like her own life. *Only in my case,* she realized, *it's movies I'm in love with—and my parents would never approve!*

Lily pushed open heavy double doors, and Rebecca entered a huge room with a glass ceiling. Light flooded across a stone patio with a carved railing and two stately urns overflowing with paper flowers. Behind the patio, the front of a mansion was painted on a large canvas backdrop. The mansion looked so real, Rebecca almost believed she could step inside. But the workings of the movie studio intruded into the illusion with wires, machines, and rows of spotlights. Cameras with round lenses were perched on tall tripods that looked as if they might walk across the floor on their own.

spotlight

"Well, doll-baby, this is it," Lily said, waving her arm expansively.

"I never heard of a ceiling made of glass," Rebecca marveled.

"It gives us lots of natural light, and we don't have to worry about the weather," Lily told her.

A burly man with a bushy red mustache ambled up to them. "And if it's dark, we've got electric lights. Being inside gives us more days of shooting," he said, "and it keeps the sets steady. Even a light breeze can make the canvas backdrops sway, and then the film looks fuzzy."

"This is Roddy Fitzgerald," Lily said, "our chief carpenter."

"A carpenter to make moving pictures?" Rebecca

asked, looking up at him in surprise.

"Sure—and who else would build the stage platforms?" Roddy replied in a lilting Irish brogue. "I also build stairs, walls, balconies, and the frames for the backdrops." He arched his thick eyebrows. "You didn't think the scenery in moving pictures was real, did you now?"

"It must be swell to be the carpenter for a motion-picture studio," Rebecca said.

"Well, it surely is different," Roddy said. "You build something and then chop it up a month later. We don't save sets because of the danger of fires. You've heard of Thomas Edison, I suppose? His moving picture studio was just down the road here, but it burned to the ground around Christmas. You can't be too careful." Roddy sighed. "I'd like to have my own business someday, and build things to last. Now, that would be grand."

Rebecca nodded, but she didn't really understand. How could working anywhere else in the world be better than here?

Don Herringbone entered the studio, his face covered with pasty makeup and his eyebrows darkened, giving him a menacing look.

"There's my wicked suitor," Lily laughed.

A curling mustache was pasted on
Don Herringbone's upper lip, and he was
dressed in a tuxedo with a silk cravat at his
neck. His hair was slicked down with
shiny brilliantine. Rebecca thought he
looked a bit oily.

"Lillian, my dear," he said. He took her hand and
lightly kissed it. "You know you're in love with me!"
Lily drew back coyly, her head turned to one side.
Rebecca was fascinated. Was this part of their act?

Just then, Max walked over. He wore rough
tweed pants with suspenders buttoned over a loose
white shirt, open at the neck. His hair fell in tousled
waves under a soft cap, and his face was the same
ghostly pale as the other players'.

"Ah, the gardener," Mr. Herringbone drawled,
sounding haughty.

"Beware this scoundrel in fancy clothes," Max
advised Lillian.

Rebecca felt a shiver of delight. Were they all
acting? Why, acting for a movie didn't seem any
different than playing with her friends and just
pretending. Rebecca could playact, too. She gestured

toward Lily with a flick of her hand and spoke in a high voice. "I'm sure such an elegant lady knows her best suitor."

"You bet I do, doll-baby," Lillian laughed.

Max coughed a little. "Come on, Rebecca," he said, steering her away from the group. "Let's find a good spot where you can sit and watch."

At one side of the room, the actresses and actors who had been on the ferry leaned against walls, sat on chairs, and perched on props. "Welcome to the garden," said an actress in a feathered hat. Rebecca recognized the ostrich plumes. This was the young woman who had been so certain that she would land a role today. "In case you can't tell," the actress said, "we're all lowly worms, just waiting to be dug up. Extras like us just wriggle around, hoping the Grand Pooh-Bah will pick us for a scene—any scene, just so we can pay the rent! Otherwise, it's move back in with Mama." The other extras groaned.

Another young actress glared at Rebecca. Her lips were painted fire-engine red and her glossy nails were long and tapered. "Are you competition, or just visiting?"

"I'm just here to watch," Rebecca assured her, sitting on a hard wooden chair with her lunch box in her lap. "I'm not an actress."

"Bet you'd like to be, though," the actress replied. Rebecca squirmed under her steady gaze. How had she guessed what Rebecca was thinking? The actress turned to the other extras. "Watch out for this one," she warned, pointing a long-nailed finger at Rebecca.

Rebecca protested. "Oh no, my family would never—"

"You'll have to be as quiet as a sleeping mouse," Max cautioned her. "L.B. has a temper, and if you cause any trouble, he'll send you out."

Rebecca nodded gravely. "I won't even breathe loudly," she promised. She gave Max's hand a squeeze. "You look really handsome," she whispered. "Lots better than Don Juan. In fact, you're the best-looking ghost I've ever seen!" Max straightened up and strode off with a swagger in his step.

CHAPTER
THREE

KIDLET
ON THE SET

A deep voice boomed across the studio. "Attention, please!"

Rebecca froze.

Stagehands, actors, and extras scampered toward a tall, lanky man holding a megaphone. His slim britches were tucked into a pair of tight boots, and he held a short leather stick. He looked like a magazine photo Rebecca had seen of an actor on horseback, but she guessed he was no actor, and no rider, either. He must be Lawrence B. Diamond, the director.

"We'll start from where we cut yesterday," he announced. "Diana," he said, gesturing to Lillian Armstrong, "find your mark!" Lily sauntered onto the patio set and stood precisely in one fixed spot at the rail. "Gus the gardener stands before her, holding up the flower," the director continued. A young man in a faded blue smock handed Max a white rose as he walked to the opposite side of the railing. Was it a real flower, or just paper?

"The villainous Rex Wentworth is spying on the young lovers," L.B. called out. Don Herringbone hunched behind a potted bush and peered out at the couple. Rebecca saw a chalked line on the floor that snaked around the patio. She could only imagine what Mama would say if Rebecca drew on the floor!

"When the camera rolls," L.B. called through his megaphone, "Gus hands Diana the rose. She breathes in its perfume and holds it against her heart. Gus points down the pathway, inviting Diana to join him. Diana, you look back nervously at the mansion. Are your parents watching? Your father would be furious if you considered marrying a man of such humble means. He might even disown you, and you would be penniless! But Gus's entreaties win you over. You step down the stairs and take his outstretched hand."

Rebecca was enthralled with the director's

REBECCA AND THE MOVIES

scenario. Max and Lily had to show the emotions their characters felt and act out a story. And they had to do it all without saying a word, because movies were silent. Their acting had to be perfect.

"As the young lovers disappear down the path, holding hands, Rex Wentworth scowls and strokes his mustache. He will not lose Diana to this lowly gardener! His crafty eyes narrow as he thinks of a plan to foil the lovers. He slinks toward the mansion to inform Diana's parents about their daughter and the gardener—and win Diana for his own!"

L.B. began pacing in front of the set. "We need more action. More drama." He tapped his riding crop against the megaphone, and the noise echoed across the silent studio. Then he hit the megaphone with a resounding whack! Rebecca flinched.

"I've got it!" he shouted. "Diana has a little sister who sees everything. She runs off to warn the couple as soon as Rex leaves." He lifted his arms in frustration. "We need a kidlet!" he wailed. "Where am I going to get a kidlet now?"

The young actress in the feathered hat rushed forward, the plumes bobbing. "I've played kid roles before," she said eagerly. "You always say I've got a girlish look." She tilted her head and propped a finger against her chin.

L.B. considered, squinting at her in the bright light. Then he shook his head. "Not for this role, Bess." The actress walked off, her eyes downcast.

Rebecca had promised Max that she wouldn't make a peep, but in the blink of an eye, everything had changed. Here was a chance to step from her ordinary life into a thrilling new world. If she thought about it too long, she would miss her chance forever.

She jumped up from her seat. "I can do it," she announced. All the extras turned to stare.

"I knew it," said the young woman with the long, shiny nails. "Another scene stealer."

"Who are you, and what are you doing on my set?" thundered L.B. At that moment, Rebecca knew why the actors called him the Grand Pooh-Bah. Her knees felt as wobbly as Mama's noodles.

Max rushed to Rebecca's side. "It just so happens I've brought the perfect little sister along," he said. He draped his arm around her shoulder, bolstering her confidence. Rebecca tried to stand tall.

The director summoned Rebecca with a

beckoning finger. The extras around her moved aside in two waves. To Rebecca it felt as if the Red Sea had parted once again, and she had to get across before it was too late. She stepped forward under L.B.'s steady gaze.

"Ever acted in a stage play?" he demanded.

If I admit the truth, he probably won't even consider putting me in the movie, she thought. But she couldn't lie. "No, sir," she gulped.

"Good!" L.B. declared. "Stage actors make lousy motion picture actors. All they want is applause ringing in their ears." He motioned Rebecca closer, and she took a few more halting steps. L.B. lifted her chin in his hand and turned her face to the right and then to the left. "Ummm," he said. "Great big eyes hiding under that spectacular hat." Now Rebecca smiled. "Aaah! Nice bright teeth!"

"She's not playing the Big Bad Wolf," Max said. "Just put a dress on her and roll 'em."

"Wardrobe!" L.B. shouted, and Mabel rushed up. "Something fancy," he ordered, "to go with this fabulous hat. And make it snappy! We've got a garden party to attend."

Mabel took Rebecca's hand and hurried her into

a room filled with racks of clothes and a sewing machine. A round platform surrounded by mirrors stood at one end. It was just like one in the tailor's shop where Papa had his pants measured.

"There's got to be something here we can use," Mabel fussed. She waved her hand toward the racks of suits and elegant dresses.

"Did you make all these?" Rebecca wondered aloud.

"I do most of the women's clothes," Mabel said. "But some things, like this cape, are bought in used clothing shops." She draped a rippling fur-trimmed cape around Rebecca's shoulders before whisking it back to the rack. "This definitely won't do for a garden party." She rifled through the racks and pulled out a silky pink gown with a softly ruffled neckline.

With Mabel's help, Rebecca stepped out of her everyday clothes and into the shimmering gown. Mabel pulled the waist tighter and looked at the effect. With a pincushion in her hand, she led Rebecca to the round platform, quickly pinned the waist, and then sewed it quickly with wide, looping stitches.

Mabel pulled out a silky pink gown with a softly ruffled neckline.

Mabel pointed to a table with a makeup kit on it. "Let's get started on your face paint." Rebecca carefully set her hat on a chair while Mabel opened a jar of cold cream. She dabbed some lightly on Rebecca's face. Then she applied pale greasepaint and drew black liner around Rebecca's eyes.

"I look like a white-faced raccoon!" Rebecca sputtered.

"Don't jiggle!" Mabel scolded. "Pucker your lips as if you were going to give me a big kiss." Rebecca puckered, and Mabel painted on lip color with a tickly soft brush. Then she fluffed Rebecca's hair. "Look at all these lovely waves. I think we can almost match Miss Armstrong's curly wig," she said. She wet a comb and pulled it through Rebecca's hair, forming springy finger curls as she went.

Finally, Mabel fitted Rebecca's hat back on carefully. "At least you arrived with *some* of your costume," she smiled.

"It was a birthday present from Max," Rebecca said. "He thought movie people would truly appreciate it."

Mabel blushed a little. "That Max sure is a charmer, ain't he?" She fluffed out Rebecca's ringlets.

"There now, you're ready to go."

Rebecca stood as still as a statue, staring at herself in the mirror. Was she really still Rebecca, or had she been transformed into a totally different girl?

There was no time to linger. Mabel handed Rebecca a frilly parasol and rushed her back to the set. The actors were lounging against the patio railing, and the camera-man was aiming his lens at the scene. "Light's perfect," he said, turning to the director. "Let's shoot."

"Ahh, here's our little miss," L.B. said, taking Rebecca's hand and leading her toward a vine-covered archway that stood just to the side of the patio. He pointed to a chalked X on the floor. "Stand on this mark," L.B. told her. "Then step under the archway. You look over and see Diana and Gus making goo-goo eyes at each other. You spy on them, and flash one of your brilliant smiles. Then you hear a sound." The director looked at her steadily. "How will the audience know you hear something?" he asked, and then he answered his own question. "You have to exaggerate every expression. Don't worry about overdoing it. Put your hand to your ear and cock your head as if you're straining to hear a sound. Then shrink back under the archway, look toward Rex, and open your eyes wide with fear! Next, crouch down and wait. When the others have gone, dash through the archway and run down the path after your sister."

Rebecca felt paler than the makeup on her face. Could she do what the director asked? There was so much to remember. At home, she had made up dozens of roles to pretend she was someone else, but this was different—this was a real moving picture!

"Let's rehearse it once without the camera," the director said as the other actors took their places on the set.

Rebecca began to go through the motions that L.B. had described. But as soon as she stepped toward the archway, he interrupted. "Watch those chalk marks! Anything outside the lines is out of the camera range. Start again," he ordered.

So that's what the chalk lines are for, Rebecca thought as she stepped onto the X and repeated the motions.

The director stopped her again. "Move more

slowly, or the film will be blurry. Every motion comes out faster when we film it."

Rebecca tried again, slowing her movements. When she looked at Max and Lily, she told herself that these were not the people she knew, but her sister Diana and Gus the gardener. She smiled.

"Bigger smile! Let's see those pearly white teeth!" the director shouted through his megaphone, his commands echoing through the studio.

Rebecca couldn't believe how hard it was to smile on demand. She knew she should be bubbling with happiness, but the smile felt false.

"Stop!" L.B. yelled. He strode over to Rebecca and bent down until they were eye to eye. Rebecca felt sure he was going to replace her with an experienced actress. She would have to step out of the dress and become a silent bystander again. But instead of sending her away, L.B. spoke to her kindly. "Got the jitters?" he asked.

Rebecca nodded. "I—I want to do it, but I don't know if I can."

"Pretend there's not another soul on this set except your sister and her beau," L.B. advised her.

Rebecca took a deep breath and went back to

her mark. Papa thought actors were lazy, but acting in a movie was hard work. Rebecca tried to forget about everything except the story as she played the scene. She exaggerated every move, remembered to stay inside the chalk lines, and at the end ran *slowly* down the path.

"You've got it!" L.B. boomed through his megaphone. "Places, everyone!" Actors froze on their marks. The cameraman turned his cap so that the visor was facing backward and put his eye close to the camera.

The director raised his megaphone and tapped it with his riding crop. "And roll!" he yelled.

Faintly, Rebecca heard the ratcheting of a crank as the cameraman turned a handle. She shut out every sound except L.B.'s shouted instructions. Suddenly, it was easy to imagine she was at a fancy garden party, about to save her sister from a nasty suitor. She forgot about being Rebecca and became the role she played, going through the motions as if she were inside the body of another girl.

"And cut!" shouted L.B. "It's a take!" He turned to the cameraman. "Get this footage developed double-quick. I want to see it today."

Rebecca awoke as if from a dream. Had she really filmed a scene in a movie?

Max put his arm around her. "A natural!" he exulted.

"Not bad for a rookie," Lily said with a warm smile.

"Talented little kidlet," L.B. remarked as he headed off the set. "See you at lunch."

CHAPTER
FOUR

MUSIC WHEREVER
SHE GOES

Still in their elegant gowns and greasepaint, Rebecca and Lily joined the rest of the crew for lunch. Their face makeup made them look chalky white, but they rubbed off the lip color so that they could eat lunch and not lip rouge. Max waved Rebecca over to where he stood in the cafeteria line.

"Gosh, Max," Rebecca fretted beside him. "Am I the only one bringing my lunch from home?"

Lily held up a small basket with a napkin folded on top. "You're going to have plenty of company today," she pointed out. "Lots of us aren't eating from the studio kitchen this week." Rebecca looked around and saw that several people were opening boxes and baskets and taking out homemade lunches.

As the cafeteria line moved forward, Lily looked at Max with surprise. "Did you know the stew they're serving today has dumplings on top?" she asked. Dumplings were made with flour and leavening, and Max surely knew they were forbidden during Passover.

Max shrugged, looking sheepish. "Of course I wasn't going to eat the dumplings. But I don't have anything else."

"Come on, you can have some of my lunch," Rebecca offered, taking his hand. "Mama always gives me more than I can eat."

As they followed Lily to a table, Don Herringbone sauntered up, his painted eyebrows making him look threatening. "Come, Lily, my dear," he said, "we'll find a private table."

"Not today," the actress answered. "I'm keeping the kidlet company."

Mr. Herringbone looked insulted. "Well! That's a fine how-de-do," he sputtered. In a quick change of mood, he pasted on a charming smile and joined two extras nearby. The actresses gazed at him adoringly.

Max pulled out a chair for Lily and then for Rebecca before sitting down next to Roddy. The carpenter unwrapped a gigantic sandwich with meat and cheese hanging out the sides.

"Meet my companion, the leftover Easter ham," Roddy said, holding up his sandwich. "I'll be keepin' it company for days to come."

Max opened Rebecca's lunch box and rummaged around. "So, what have you got?" he asked. "Are you sure there's enough for me?"

"I've got plenty for both of us," said Roddy, offering half of his bulging sandwich. Max started to reach for it, but then with a guilty glance at Rebecca and Lily he quickly declined.

"Max!" Rebecca exclaimed. "You wouldn't really eat a sandwich on Passover, would you? Especially one with ham!" Jewish people never ate pork products, whether it was Passover or not. It just wasn't *kosher*.

Max's cheeks turned red, even through his heavy makeup. It was the first time Rebecca had ever seen him look embarrassed.

"Poor Max," Lily crooned. "Don't you have

anyone to cook for you?" She opened her basket. "I've got enough to share." Lily took out small glass containers of herring salad, Russian beet and potato salad, and orange sections. Rebecca began to spread out her lunch on the table, as well. Just as she unwrapped her matzo, she saw Lily take some from her basket.

Rebecca grinned. "You have matzo, too!"

Lily nodded toward L.B. "Take a gander at the Grand Pooh-Bah himself." The director was munching on squares of matzo spread with jam.

Max took a bite of Lily's herring salad. "Delicious," he murmured.

Lily gave Max a warm smile. "At Passover, I pull out all my mother's recipes. She might not like my job, but she can't criticize my cooking."

Rebecca expected Max to offer a joking response, but instead, silence fell over the table. Max was so quiet when Lily was around, thought Rebecca. He definitely wasn't himself.

Roddy stood up. "I think we need to liven this place up a bit," he announced. A phonograph sat on an empty table, with a stack of records piled next to it. Roddy cranked the handle, and a scratchy voice sang from the speaker, "Down by the old mill stream, where I first met you . . ."

Max reached for Rebecca's hand and made a gentlemanly bow. "Shall we dance, *mademoiselle?*"

Here was the Max that Rebecca knew—always full of delightful surprises. She took his hand and struggled to follow his graceful box step. Soon the music led her along, and they swirled between the tables. Rebecca's fancy party gown swished with every turn.

"So," Max said as they glided along, "how do you like being an actress?"

"It's wonderful," Rebecca sighed. "I forgot I was me when I started acting. It seemed as if I actually became someone else. It's such fun pretending to be a different girl leading a completely different life!"

"Acting lets you shed your everyday skin and try on a new one," Max said. "There aren't many chances in life to do that." He twirled her around as the song ended. Roddy replaced the record with a ragtime piano tune.

"It's Scott Joplin!" Max exclaimed. "Let's keep dancing."

But Rebecca thought she had a better idea. "I've

got to catch my breath," she fibbed, pulling Max to the table. "Why don't you dance with Lily?"

"Why, Max, I thought you'd never ask," Lily said gaily. Max stood silently, as if he were rooted to the floor. With a private wink at Rebecca, Lily took Max's hand and led him away from the crowded tables. Rebecca nibbled her lunch and watched as Max swung Lily around the floor to the fast-paced music. Max was a smooth dancer, and Lily kept up with every move. When the record ended, they flopped down on their chairs, laughing.

"I didn't know you were such a swell dancer," Lily complimented Max.

"There are a lot of things you don't know about me," Max said softly. "But you could find out." Lily batted her dark eyelashes.

Rebecca stifled a giggle as she unwrapped the leftover party cookies. She offered them to Max and Lily and then chose a macaroon for herself.

"These treats are from Rebecca's birthday party on Saturday," Max explained. "She is now an actress at the tender age of ten years and one day!"

"Happy birthday, doll-baby!" Lily said. "You're having quite a celebration."

"It's my best birthday ever," Rebecca agreed. She pushed the cookies to the center of the table. "Here, Max, you and Lily finish these. I'm going to see if Roddy will let me crank the phonograph."

Roddy let Rebecca choose the next record and wind up the turntable. As the music played, Rebecca stole glances at Max and Lily. They didn't seem to be talking much, but Max was making the same "goo-goo eyes" as in the scene on the patio. Only this time, Rebecca didn't think Max was acting.

Don Herringbone had noticed the couple, too. After one scowling glance, he left the room in a huff.

❧

The afternoon was filled with more filming. "I want to get all the scenes with the kidlet in them," L.B. said. "We've only got one day."

Rebecca sighed. She wondered if she'd ever have a chance to be in a motion picture again.

The crew moved to a different set. Rebecca stepped onto a low platform with a simple backdrop of painted trees. Would it really look like a wooded path in the film?

She concentrated on her scene. "Di-an-a!" she

59

called, moving her mouth in exaggerated motion. When the couple turned, she imitated Rex spying on them, pretending to stroke a mustache. Diana and Gus raised their eyebrows in alarm. Rebecca pointed back toward the mansion, where Rex had gone. Diana sagged against Gus in shock, and he fanned her face with his handkerchief. When Diana recovered, he knelt on one knee, clasped his hands together, and implored Diana to marry him. She batted her eyelashes and nodded as Rebecca gazed at them with a joyful smile.

"Freeze!" shouted L.B., and the trio stood stock still. "And fade! It's a take."

Lily hugged Rebecca. "You were perfect!" she told her. "Your face is so expressive. I worked on that for years, and it comes so naturally to you."

"Now," Max said, "go turn yourself back into Rebecca in the dressing room, and take a nice break. Later we'll go watch the rushes."

"Rushes?" Rebecca asked.

"That's movie talk for film that's been rushed into development," Max explained. "The camera-man develops it in his chemical soup, and later this afternoon we all get to see how it looks. It's hardly ever what you expect!"

Back in Lily's dressing room, Rebecca carefully hung the silky pink gown on a hanger. Borrowing one of Lily's satin robes, she rubbed cold cream on her face and washed it clean. Soon she was back to herself again, in her own dress, cotton stockings, and sturdy shoes. Trying to hang on to the magic of the day, she left her hair in ringlets and kept on her hat. One of the extras brought in two cups and a pot of tea, and Rebecca and Lily spent the rest of the afternoon sipping, talking, and thumbing through moving picture magazines. Rebecca felt deliciously grown-up. She could hardly believe she was the same Rebecca who was nine years old only two days before.

At last a rhythmic knock sounded at the dressing room door. *Rap-rap-a-tap-tap*—

"That's Max," Rebecca said, jumping up. "He always does that." She gave the two responding taps, and Max opened the door.

With one actress on each arm, Max walked Rebecca and Lily down a flight of stairs to a dim, windowless basement room. One wall had white canvas stretched across it. Actors and crew members sat in rows of chairs facing the canvas, and a movie projector buzzed at the back of the room.

"Almost ready," said the cameraman, looping the film along a series of sprockets in the projector.

Don Herringbone came in, accompanied by a pretty young woman who Rebecca guessed was another actress. They took seats apart from the others, talking softly with their heads close together. Max had been right—Mr. Herringbone loved the ladies. All of them!

L.B. entered the room with a fat cigar stuck in his mouth, and silence fell over the group. The director closed the door, plunging the room into complete darkness. Rebecca felt the same thrill she had felt when she watched the Charlie Chaplin film. "Roll it!" L.B. called through his teeth.

The projector whirred and a flickering light came on. A close shot of Lily opened to fill the canvas screen. She stood at the balcony, surrounded by lush flowers.

"There wasn't any flower garden when that scene was shot!" Rebecca whispered to Max.

 "Glass plates," Max whispered back. "The flowers are painted on a piece of glass, and the glass is placed in front of

the camera lens. It's motion picture magic. The scene in the woods will have a glass plate, too, with leafy trees all around."

So that's what glass plates were. Rebecca would never have imagined that the flower garden would look so real.

Max entered the scene, holding the white rose and wooing his sweetheart. In a moment, Rebecca saw a young girl in a flowing gown walking toward a vine-covered archway. *That's me!* she thought, her breath catching in her throat. But the girl on the screen looked nothing like her. Rebecca watched the film version of herself go through the scene, her dark eyes revealing each emotion to the audience. There were a few close-up shots where she looked larger than life. In other scenes, the audience saw just a side view with her face partly hidden by her hat.

"Looks good," L.B. announced as the film footage flickered to an end. "Put it in the can."

Lily shook Rebecca's hand. "Congratulations, doll-baby. Now you're a real player."

"That's me!" Rebecca thought, her breath catching in her throat.

Rebecca took one last look through the gate as they waited for the bus back to the ferry. "Even if I never get to be in another motion picture, at least my name will be on the screen for this one." Max and Lily looked at her without a word. "Won't it?" Rebecca asked.

Max put his hand on Rebecca's shoulder. "I'm afraid not," he said. "Banbury Cross Studios just started listing the names of the main actors and actresses on the screen. Before that, none of the players' names were listed in the movie. In fact, this is the first time *my* name will appear on the screen."

"Right up there with mine," Lily said, squeezing Max's arm playfully.

"Gosh, my friends will never know that's me in the movie," Rebecca said. Then she reconsidered. "On the other hand, it's probably good that Bubbie will never know. She'd hate having another actor in the family!" Rebecca clapped her hand over her mouth. She hadn't meant to insult Max.

"You mean my own relatives don't respect my

theatrical pursuits?" he said, gasping in mock surprise. Then he patted Rebecca's arm. "Don't worry, I already know exactly what they think. They've told me enough times!"

"Oh, Max, I'm sorry," Rebecca stammered. "Everyone in the family loves you."

"I know." Max shrugged. "They just don't love my job."

Lily nodded in sympathy. "My parents think actors are simply wicked! When they were growing up, it wasn't respectable for women to be in show business. They tried everything to get me to become a bookkeeper. Still, Mama admits that they go to every picture I'm in."

"You see?" Max said. "I just know motion pictures are going to sweep America. There's never been anything like them! And mark my words—if you're a successful actor, people will admire and respect you."

Rebecca imitated Bubbie's frown and accent. "A respectable young lady in a moving pit-cher? *Oy vey!*" Then she grew serious. "I think being an actress would be better than any job in the world—even better than working in the shoe store or being a teacher, as Papa wants me to be." Rebecca sat down on the bus with Max beside her, and Lily took a seat behind them. "Do you think my family would ever let me be an actress?" Rebecca asked.

Max hesitated before answering. "It wouldn't be easy for them to accept, Rebecca—especially your grandparents."

Rebecca mulled over Max's words. She was heading back to her ordinary life—but she had discovered something inside herself, and she would never be the same. Now she had a dream of acting in motion pictures. Hadn't Max called her "a natural"? Even L.B., the Grand Pooh-Bah himself, had said she was talented.

Rebecca wanted her family to be proud of her always, but if she became an actress, they wouldn't be—at least not at first, and maybe not ever. Rebecca thought back over the past two days. She had given up her wish for a birthday cake when she thought it might be wrong. But it would be much harder to give up her dream of becoming an actress. And as it turned out, having a birthday cake during Passover wasn't wrong after all. Maybe being an actress wasn't wrong, either.

Rebecca glanced over at Max and Lily. They had faced their families' disapproval to do what they loved. Would she?

The actors and crew had nearly all settled onto the bus when Roddy climbed aboard carrying a big box. He stopped by Rebecca's seat. "I heard you reciting the rhyme about Banbury Cross this morning," he said. "You know the rest of it—'With rings on her fingers and bells on her toes, she shall have music wherever she goes.'" He slipped a paper band from one of L.B.'s cigars onto her finger. "I didn't have bells for your toes," he chuckled, "but a lass such as yourself should have music wherever you go." He set the box at her feet.

Rebecca peered inside and saw a shiny red horn. "A phonograph!"

"L.B. wanted you to have a little souvenir from the Prop Room," Roddy said. "Consider it payment for a fine day's work."

"Thank you," Rebecca breathed. Her very own phonograph! She couldn't wait to show Rose.

Darkness enveloped the ferry as Rebecca stepped aboard. Max pointed to the sky. "Where can you always see shooting stars?" he asked. When

Rebecca couldn't guess, he slapped his knee. "Why, at a cowboy movie!"

Rebecca laughed. Good old Max—always joking.

The New York skyline grew closer, sparkling with lights. Rebecca was tired, but she was too excited to rest. She looked around at all the actors and crew on the ferry, fixing them in her memory. She hoped she would see them again someday. Above her, she saw millions of stars glittering in the night sky. Maybe one day, she too would be a star, flickering brightly on a silver screen.

LOOKING BACK

GROWING UP
IN 1914

A Jewish family of 1917 with nine children

When Rebecca was growing up, families tended to be much larger than they are today. Rebecca's family, with five children, would not have been considered a large family at all. Some families had as many as fifteen children!

Children in immigrant neighborhoods like Rebecca's did not have as many toys to play with as children do today. In a cramped city apartment there was not much room for playing, and outside there was no lawn or backyard to play in, either. Instead, city children played out on the sidewalk or in the street. Girls

The game of leapfrog needed no equipment and little space to play.

A street game of stickball

like Rebecca
played sidewalk
games such as
jacks, jump
rope, and hop-
scotch. A boy like Victor would have enjoyed *stickball*,
a simple form of baseball that could be played in the
street.

In the days before television, the street was a fun
place to play for another reason: it was entertaining,
almost like a reality TV show. The crowded, busy streets
of the Lower East Side always had interesting things
to see. You could watch neighbors coming and going,
shoppers haggling with pushcart peddlers, or the
policeman on his beat. You could pet the iceman's horse
and maybe get a free chip of ice to suck on a hot day.

*Before refrigerators,
ice was delivered by
horse and wagon.*

*The entryway of
a movie theater*

Even more
fun than watching
the street life was
watching a moving
picture, as movies
were called then.
By 1914, feature
films were about
ten years old—and already extremely popular. Movies
were silent, so theaters had a piano player who played
along with the movie, adding the right kind of music for
each scene. If the movie needed
words to explain the action,
writing appeared on the screen
to show what the actors were
saying.

*One theater showed this image before
the movie started so that people would
know how to behave during the movie.*

In Rebecca's day, a child's
movie ticket cost about five
cents, and you would get to see
several films: a short comedy,
a longer drama, and a short
newsreel, or documentary. Some
theaters were large and fancy,
while others were just old stores
with the walls painted black and a bedsheet for a screen.
But people didn't care. They just couldn't get enough of
movies!

The earliest films did not list credits for the actors.

John Barrymore moved from stage to screen acting. His granddaughter is today's actress Drew Barrymore.

In fact, most of the public thought movie acting was a low art form. Stage actors earned more respect. However, movie actors soon earned more money. By the time Rebecca would have been a young woman, movie acting was considered a respectable way to make a living.

The most popular movie actresses of Rebecca's time were Mary Pickford and Theda Bara. Nicknamed "America's Sweetheart," Mary Pickford was famous for her long golden curls and the lovable characters she played. Theda Bara was the opposite. She had long black hair and was known as "The Vamp," but playing wicked characters didn't keep her from being hugely popular.

MARY PICKFORD
IN
REBECCA OF
SUNNYBROOK FARM
FROM THE PLAY BY KATE DOUGLAS WIGGIN AND CHARLOTTE THOMPSON
SCENARIO BY FRANCIS MARION DIRECTED BY MARSHALL NEILAN
ARTCRAFT PICTURES CORPORATION

Girls loved reading movie magazines, which told all about their favorite movie stars.

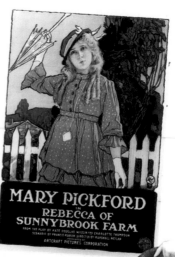

Theda Bara

Audiences also loved child actors. Little
Helen Badgley started out acting in movies
as a baby, and by 1914, she was a big star,
even though she was only five years old.
Two years later, she had to drop out of a
movie because she had lost her two front
teeth and had to wait until new ones grew in!

Most movie studios started out in
New York or nearby New Jersey, but the
studios had already discovered Hollywood.
California's mild weather allowed directors
to shoot outdoors, where the light
was better, all year round. Within a

Mary Pickford
shooting a movie
in southern
California

few years, the studios moved to southern California, where they remain today.

Most of today's big film studios—including Paramount, Warner Brothers, Universal, Fox, and MGM—got their start in Rebecca's time, and they were started by Jewish immigrants. American businessmen shied away from the risky new business of movie-making, but Jewish immigrants were hungry for new opportunities. They also knew how much Americans loved show business, and they realized that movies could draw much larger audiences—and earn more money—than live theater productions. They had a hunch that movies would soon be the most popular form of entertainment in America. They were right!

Today, girls still love watching movies.

Glossary

bubbie *(BUH-bee)*—**Grandmother** in Yiddish

bubeleh *(BUH-beh-leh)*—the Yiddish way to say **darling** or **sweetie**

entrez *(on-tray)*—the French word for **enter**

kosher *(KOH-sher)*—a Yiddish word meaning **fit to eat** under the Jewish dietary laws

mademoiselle *(mad-mwah-zel)*—French for **young lady**

matzo *(MOT-zuh)*—the Yiddish word for a large, square **cracker** eaten instead of bread during Passover. It can also be ground into matzo meal and made into matzo balls for soup, or used instead of flour in baking.

mazel tov *(MAH-zl tof)*—Yiddish for **congratulations!**

oy vey *(oy vay)*—a Yiddish exclamation, meaning **oh, dear!**

seder *(SAY-der)*—a Hebrew word for the **ceremonial dinner** held on the first night or the first and second nights of Passover

A SNEAK PEEK AT

Rebecca

TO THE RESCUE

A day at Coney Island—what could be more exciting! If only bossy Victor would stop ruining all Rebecca's fun.

They moved on, past shooting galleries with rifles aimed at mechanical ducks, and tossing games of all kinds. Wonderful prizes lined the top shelf in each booth, and Rebecca thought it must be swell to go home with a prize. Suddenly a row of Kewpie dolls caught her eye.

"Oh," she cried, pointing to the pot-bellied dolls. "Just look at those impish eyes and that cute tuft of hair. Remember those Kewpies on the cover of my school notebook?" she asked Ana. "I just adore Kewpies."

"Step right up, little lady," cried the barker. "All these little babies want is a good home. For one nickel, you can't lose." He turned to a pyramid of wooden pins set up behind him. "Just knock over these pins with a baseball and you can choose your prize. Everybody's a winner!"

Rebecca hesitated. She didn't have much money, and the game cost five cents. "Where in the world could you get your very own Kewpie for just one buffalo nickel?" asked the barker. Rebecca knew she couldn't buy one for twice as much. Lined up beside the dolls were baseball gloves, boxed cigars, and plush teddy bears. She would definitely choose a Kewpie.

"You could never win this game," Victor scoffed. "You couldn't hit the side of a tenement house with a baseball." A group of boys standing around the booth began to laugh. Rebecca felt her anger rising.

The barker glanced at the boys. "At Coney Island, everyone gets to do something new," he declared. "And you have three tries. Give it a whirl, little lady, and the Kewpie's yours."

"Let's go," Victor said. "We're wasting time."

"You think that only boys can throw?" Rebecca demanded. "What about hopscotch? You need good aim for that. Girls can throw—and aim, too."

"What about hopscotch?" mimicked one of the boys standing nearby.

"*Hopscotch?*" his friends echoed. They doubled over with laughter, slapping each other on the back.

They'll stop laughing if I win, thought Rebecca. With three chances, she was sure she could do it. She pulled a knotted handkerchief from her sash and counted out five pennies. She plunked them on the counter.

The barker set three balls on the counter. "Go to it, sweetheart."

Rebecca picked up the first ball. She eyed the stacked pins carefully, took aim, and threw with all her might. The ball whacked into the backboard without even grazing the pins. *I can do it,* she thought, steadying her nerves. *I have two more tries.*

Rebecca picked up the second ball and felt its weight. Maybe she didn't need to throw as hard as she had thought. She took a step back and threw a gentle toss. The pin at the very top of the pyramid wobbled but stayed where it was.

"You call that throwing?" one of the boys jeered. He turned to his friends. "She throws just like a girl!"

"She *is* a girl," retorted another, and they all whooped with laughter.

Rebecca's heart was beating out of her chest. It throbbed high into her throat and up to her ears. Her face felt hot. She picked up the last ball, and no one made a sound. This time she used her whole arm, the way she had seen Victor pitch. The ball hit the pins. The top rows tumbled down with a thunderous crash, and the twins gasped. Rebecca

The top two rows tumbled down with a thunderous crash,
and Rebecca thought she had done it.

thought she had done it—but two pins in the bottom row were left standing.

"Good try," consoled the barker. "And no one leaves without a prize." He handed her a small metal pin with a grinning Funny Face on it. The face that had looked so amusing when she arrived at Steeplechase now seemed to be mocking her. "Now that you've got the hang of it," the barker said, "why not try again? This time you're sure to win that Kewpie."

Lily had said that everyone felt foolish at Coney Island, and it was all in fun. But Rebecca felt completely humiliated, and it didn't seem fun or funny.

"You wasted five whole cents," Victor pointed out. "You should have listened to me."

"Leave me alone!" Rebecca blurted out. Tears welled in her eyes, and she turned away.

"Aww, don't take it so hard," Victor said. "I'm sorry I teased you. It's just that you don't have any practice throwing a baseball."

"Sure," Rebecca said. "Only *boys* can play baseball, right? Girls can't do anything!" A few

84

people turned and stared. They were grinning as wide as the Funny Face, and Rebecca thought they looked horrid.

"I'm leaving," she said. "I'll meet you by the carousel later."

"You can't go off alone," Sadie said. "We promised to stay together."

"And I've got the tickets!" Victor reminded her, but Rebecca didn't care.

Ana caught her arm. "I'll go with you," she offered. "Then we won't really be breaking our promise, because *we'll* be together."

As the girls started to walk away, Rebecca heard the barker calling out, "Here you go, hot shot, give it a try. You can't lose!" Rebecca glanced back and saw Victor pick up a ball. Then she heard wooden pins crashing and cheers from the boys hanging around the booth. Victor must have won with just one throw.

READ ALL OF REBECCA'S STORIES,
available at bookstores and *americangirl.com.*

MEET REBECCA
When Rebecca finds a way to earn money,
she keeps it a secret from her family.

REBECCA AND ANA
Rebecca is going to sing for the whole school.
Will cousin Ana ruin her big moment?

CANDLELIGHT FOR REBECCA
Rebecca's family is Jewish.
Is it wrong for Rebecca to make a
Christmas decoration in school?

REBECCA AND THE MOVIES
At the movie studio with cousin Max,
Rebecca finds herself in front of the camera!

REBECCA TO THE RESCUE
A day at Coney Island brings more
excitement and thrills than Rebecca expected.

CHANGES FOR REBECCA
When Rebecca sees injustice around her, she
takes to the streets and speaks her mind.